Janine.

by Maryann Cocca-Leffler

ALBERT WHITMAN & COMPANY
CHICAGO, ILLINOIS

To my daughter, Janine. Thank You.
To children everywhere,
Love who you are.

Library of Congress Cataloging-in-Publication data
is on file with the publisher.

Text and pictures copyright © 2015 Maryann Cocca-Leffler
Published in 2015 by Albert Whitman & Company
ISBN 978-0-8075-3754-1

Printed in China.
10 9 8 7 6 5 4 3 2 1 HH 18 17 16 15 14

For more information about Albert Whitman & Company,
visit our web site at www.albertwhitman.com.

Join the Party!
Everyone is invited.

www.JaninesParty.com

Visit Maryann at
www.MaryannCoccaLeffler.com

This is
Janine.

She is one of a kind.

She sings aloud on the bus,

If you're happy and you know it...

talks to her imaginary friend,

It's your turn.

and remembers things— lots of things.

She reads the dictionary
when others are playing

"Can I come?"

"I do!
It's spectacular!"

"No one says big
words like that!"

"No one hangs out with them!"

"I do!"

"I do! I do!

And I made up a great cheer..."

"Then you are NOT coming to MY party!"

WANTS
TO MY

"Spectacular!"